The Zoo Switcheroo

Enjoy More Great S.O.S. Adventures!

By Alan Katz

Illustrated by Alex Lopez

HARPER

An Imprint of HarperCollins*Publishers*

To Rose, whose superpowers amaze and delight

—Alan Katz

Library of Congress Control Number: 2020937707

ISBN 978-0-06-290934-3 — ISBN 978-0-06-290935-0 (pbk.)

Typography by Corina Lupp

20 21 22 23 24   PC/LSCC   10 9 8 7 6 5 4 3 2 1

❖

First Edition

TABLE OF CONTENTS

CHAPTER 1

Field Trip!

HELLO, KIDS OF 311B.
TODAY WE'RE GOING TO THE ZOO.
IT'S A CHANCE TO GREET THE
ANTELOPE AND ASK EACH ONE,
"WHAT'S GNU?"

The second graders of 311B could always rely on Mrs. Baltman for a funny Monday sign. And they especially enjoyed this one, because it was both hilarious *and* true. They were taking a class field trip to the city zoo!

Milton Worthy walked to his desk and blurted out to no one in particular:

"I'm ready to do schoolwork. What? No work

2

today? Field trip? Oh, okay, if you insist. I'll just put my schoolbooks away."

Milton laughed. Wow, did he crack himself up.

"Hello, everyone. As you know, today is our long-awaited class trip," Mrs. Baltman said. "We will be leaving soon; please take your seats."

"Please take our seats *to the zoo*?" Milton asked her. "Won't they be hard to carry around?"

Mrs. Baltman thought about what Milton had said. Then she started laughing. A lot. It was the kind of laugh that teachers don't usually laugh in front of their students.

And that made the kids laugh too. It was the kind of laugh that *kids* don't usually laugh in front of their teachers.

Everyone was still laughing as Mrs. Baltman's classroom phone rang. She answered it and said, "Ha-ha—hello?—ha-ha."

The person on the other end of the phone must have said something very serious. Because Mrs. Baltman abruptly said, "Oh my!"

Then her eyes darted around the room, and . . .

. . . she started coughing.

COUGH! COUGH!

And coughing. And coughing. The kind of coughing that would get her a starring role in a cough drop commercial.

But this wasn't a commercial. It was a classroom.

Everyone stopped laughing.

Milton looked at his teacher. Then he followed her eyes to where the class kept Noah, their pet ferret.

Noah was inside the cage, mindlessly gumming some num-nums.

Milton was confused. He knew that the last time Mrs. Baltman coughed like that, it was because Noah had escaped and tried to take over the world.

But the cage was locked. The ferret was

gumming. All seemed right with the world. Until . . .

. . . a shadow appeared in the classroom doorway.

It was the shadow of someone Milton immediately recognized.

Someone he knew very well.

So well, in fact, that he'd had breakfast with her that very morning.

It was . . .

. . . none other than . . .

Take a guess. Who do you think it is?

CHAPTER 2

Something Is Up

. . . Milton's mother, Rose Worthy.

Mrs. Worthy was a full-time mom and a sometimes substitute teacher.

She was also a superhero: a proud member of the Society of Substitutes. As part of the S.O.S., she was

experienced in saving the world from ferrets and other classroom creatures that turned evil.

Milton's mom stepped into the classroom and whispered a few words to Mrs. Baltman. Mrs. Baltman nodded (while still coughing), and she waved goodbye to the kids and left the room.

Now Milton was really confused. He couldn't see any problem or threat. So why was his mother taking over the class?

"Good morning, everyone," Mrs. Worthy said as she wrote her name on the board. "Mrs. Baltman isn't feeling well and had to go home. I will be taking over for today. But don't worry; we will still be going to the zoo."

What is happening? Milton asked himself.

"Please line up at the door," Mrs. Worthy said. "Bring your lunch bags, and let's leave the classroom in an orderly fashion."

The kids did as Mrs. Worthy had requested. Only one of them left the line—Milton ran ahead to question his mother.

"What's going on?" Milton whispered to Mom. "Why are you here?"

Mrs. Worthy leaned in and quietly said, "Milty, Chief Chiefman at headquarters just got a C.T. of an F.W.D.A."

"Oh, a C.T. of an F.W.D.A.," Milton whispered back.

"Indeed," his mother replied.

"Um, can Y.O.U. tell M.E. what that I.S.?" Milton asked.

Mrs. Worthy smiled.

"A credible threat of a ferret world domination attempt," she told the boy.

"Uh-oh."

"Yes, uh-oh," Mrs. Worthy said. "I'm very worried. Something is up. Something is definitely going down."

Milton was puzzled as to how something could be up and going down at the same time. But he was glad his mother was there to protect everyone as they boarded the bus.

Milton found it strange that Fritz the bus driver didn't greet the kids as he usually did on class field trips. Instead, he was facing away from the door, busily fussing with the side-view mirror.

There was a flurry of activity as the kids filed onto

the bus and into the rows. Those in the back wanted to be in the front. Those on the aisle preferred window seats. And Sarah Rosario made Morgan Zhou and Max Goen play rock, paper, scissors to determine who'd be lucky enough to sit with her.

Milton had a lot on his mind. He plopped into the seat next to his mother and kept peppering her with questions.

Milton was still puzzled. He was also more than a little concerned. He sat quietly on the ride to the zoo, which, by the way, was the bumpiest, bounciest, herky-jerkiest ride ever.

When they pulled into the zoo parking lot, Fritz immediately ran off the bus. That seemed

strange. But what seemed even stranger was what Milton saw moments later. It was a scene far worse than he had dared to imagine . . .

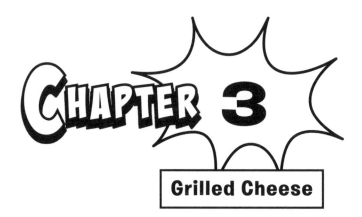

Grilled Cheese

Absolute, total chaos!

PLEASE
DON'T FEED
THE ~~ANIMALS~~
PEOPLE

Quite simply, the cages were empty and the zoo animals were running amok. Sloths were slithering. Leopards were loitering. Walruses were making a getaway. (It was a slow getaway, but still a getaway.)

And as for the lions, tigers, and bears . . . oh my!

"Mom! Look! Mom?" Milton yelled to his mother, who had seen the action and scurried to the back of the bus.

While the kids were busy watching the out-of-control animals through the bus windows, Mrs. Worthy crouched low in the last row of seats and placed her portable, folding, wireless S.O.S. transmitter helmet on her head.

As quietly as possible, Mrs. Worthy contacted Chief Chiefman and told him what was going on. The chief was upset but not surprised.

"I'm upset but I'm not surprised," he said. "This is proof of the C.T. of an F.W.D.A. Evil ferrets can be *so* evil."

"But, Chief," Mrs. Worthy said, "Noah, the evilest ferret of them all, was safely back in his classroom cage gumming num-nums. He's nowhere in sight."

"Agent W., as sure as I'm here in S.O.S. head-quarters in a top secret location on the corner of Third and Main," the chief said, "Noah is on the loose and behind all this."

"So what do we do?" Mrs. Worthy asked.

"We think," said the chief. "We think, and we hope. We think, we hope, and we eat grilled cheese."

"Why do we eat grilled cheese?" Mrs. Worthy asked him.

"I happen to like grilled cheese," the chief responded. "I sometimes eat it when I think and hope."

Meanwhile, in row seventeen, Morgan couldn't help but notice that Mrs. Worthy was speaking into her transmitter helmet.

"Hey, Milton," she said. "Your mom's doing her superhero thing again, huh?"

"Yeah," Milton told her. "I think she's calling the chief."

Mrs. Worthy's transmitter helmet battery was running low. (The folding helmet models usually don't have great battery life.) She struggled to hear the chief's words:

"*Ker-zap?*" Mrs. Worthy repeated. "Chief? Hello, Chief?"

The helmet battery was out of power. The chief hadn't *said* "ker-zap"—it was the sound the dying transmitter made.

Mrs. Worthy found Milton staring out the bus window at the rampaging rhinos and filled him in on what had happened. Morgan heard too.

"We need to get the animals back into their cages," Mrs. Worthy said. "But how . . . ?"

"Yes, how?" Morgan repeated, adding herself to the secret conversation. Mrs. Worthy knew Morgan and figured she could be helpful, so she didn't mind.

"Yes, how?" Milton echoed. "How, how, how, how, how?"

"You can stop how-ing, Milton," his superhero mother said. "After hearing the chief talk about grilled cheese, I think I have the answer . . ."

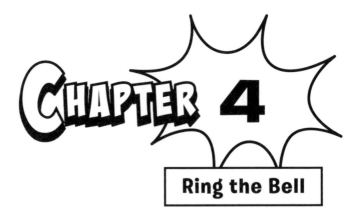

CHAPTER 4

Ring the Bell

"Look! That zebra is selling helium balloons to the buffalo!" David Tessler yelled as the kids continued watching the rampage from inside the bus.

"The owl stopped yelling 'Whooo' and is yelling 'Whyyy?'," Sarah noted.

"And there's an ape totally mucking up the Monkeyland Gift Shop!" Max added.

Everyone watched the animal antics, amazed. Everyone except Milton and Morgan. They

leaned in to hear Mrs. Worthy's plan.

"Listen," Mrs. Worthy whispered to her son and to Morgan. "Whenever we've been to the zoo, they ring a bell at feeding time, right?"

"Right," Milton said.

"And if there's one thing animals like better than running wild, it's feeding time. Am I right?"

"You are right!" Morgan agreed.

"So . . . we just have to convince the animals that it's feeding time, and they'll return to their cages."

"But . . . the next feeding time isn't until noon," Milton said. "And it's only ten thirty."

"Can sheep tell time?" Mrs. Worthy asked him. "Does a giraffe ever say, 'Wake me at a quarter to three'? They eat when the bell rings!"

"My mother's right!" Milton exclaimed. "Good thinking, Mom . . ."

"Thanks, Milty," she said.

"But . . . how do we get the feeding time bell to ring?" Morgan wanted to know.

"Just leave that to me," Mrs. Worthy told her.

Mrs. Worthy stuck out her left hand and flipped the stone on her wedding ring. Yes, the front of the stone was a handy-dandy ferret decoder. But what she needed at the moment was located on the back of the stone: a sure-fire sound effects generator.

"My wedding ring is preprogrammed with seven thousand four hundred and twelve sound effects," she told Milton and Morgan. "One feeding time signal, coming right up!"

Mrs. Worthy thrust her left hand out the bus window and pressed the stone with her right hand.

"There!" she said, smiling.

"I don't hear anything!" Milton said. "It must not be working."

"It's working perfectly," Mrs. Worthy assured him. "Animals can hear sounds that humans can't. My ring is sending out a signal that alerts the animals without scaring the humans in the zoo."

"Very cool, Mrs. W.," Morgan said. "Very cool indeed."

What was even cooler than the silent signal was the effect it had on the animals. All at once, they stopped stampeding, charging, dashing, sprinting, and selling helium balloons. Instead, every creature on the loose followed the bees and made a beeline for their cages and other enclosures.

The zookeepers chased after the animals. And as soon as they were in their cages, the zookeepers made sure to lock them in nice and tight. Within minutes, order was restored at the

zoo. The crisis was over.

"All clear," Mrs. Worthy hollered out to a nearby zookeeper.

And the zookeeper flashed the international sign for *the animals are all back in the cages and it's safe to come out*—a big thumbs-up! "All clear," she said.

"Terrific," Mrs. Worthy said with a sigh of relief. And then she turned to the class and announced, "All is calm at the zoo now!"

But was it?

CHAPTER 5

Driver-Napped!

Mrs. Worthy walked to the front of the bus and
watched as all the kids stepped down onto the

sidewalk. She wished that Fritz the bus driver had been there to help, but he was nowhere to be found.

After the last of the kids had left the bus, Mrs. Worthy plugged her transmitter helmet into the dashboard charger. Then she joined the kids on the sidewalk.

"Attention, please," she said to the class. "We've had quite an unusual trip, but Zookeeper Alice is here to show us around. Let's all be on our best behavior now that everything is calm and peaceful."

"Except for that incredibly loud banging coming from the luggage compartment," David Tessler pointed out.

"Yes, except for that incredibly loud banging coming from the luggage compartment," Mrs. Worthy agreed. "Wait . . . *loud banging*?"

Mrs. Worthy told the class that they should follow Zookeeper Alice to start the tour. She added that she'd check out the noise and catch up with them in a few minutes.

Everyone happily went with the zookeeper, except for Milton and Morgan. They stayed behind in case Mrs. Worthy needed their help. Which she did, because . . .

. . . when Mrs. Worthy ran to the compartment, she opened it to reveal . . . Fritz the bus driver! He was sitting there in nothing but his undies!

Fritz scampered out of the luggage compartment. "I've been driver-napped!" he told them breathlessly. "By a ferret! A very mean ferret. He stole my uniform, and it really didn't fit him well. Frankly, I don't even know how he did up all the buttons, you know, since ferrets don't have thumbs. He forced me into the luggage compartment"—and this is when Fritz really lost

it—"and . . . and . . . and he *drove* the bus!"

"That probably explains why the ride was so bumpy," Milton noted.

"You think it was bumpy for *you*," Fritz exclaimed. "Try taking that ride while bouncing around the luggage compartment in your underwear!"

"No thank you," Milton told him.

"Noah!" Mrs. Worthy said through gritted teeth. "I don't know how he did it, but it has to be Noah!" Mrs. Worthy sprang into action. She hopped back onto the bus and put her transmitter helmet on her head. Fortunately, the bus had been running and even a few minutes of the dashboard charger gave the helmet enough power to allow her to contact headquarters.

Speaking quickly, she told the chief what had happened. Once again, he was upset but not surprised.

And what he said in response left Mrs. Worthy both upset *and* surprised . . .

Evil Detector 3000

The sad fact was, Noah had gotten free! The creature that Milton had seen at school mindlessly gumming his num-nums was actually a robotic ferret. Mrs. Worthy had heard about the Electro-Replace-a-Ferret Model 602, but had never actually seen one in action. (Model 602 featured the auto-gumming setting! Brilliant! Evil, but brilliant!)

What was even worse, though, was that Noah had been the one who had caused all

REAL
FERRET
EYES

REAL
FERRET LIPS

FULL
ULTRA-
BLINK
ACTION
EYES

AUTO
NUM-NUM
GUMMING
ACTION

REAL FERRET
LIMBS

GEAR-DRIVEN
SPEED-O LIMBS

the mayhem. He had scurried off the bus and opened all the cages. He wanted the zoo animals to join his quest for world domination!

Fortunately, the signal Mrs. Worthy had sent to announce a fake feeding time had restored order. But that was only a temporary solution. Because it was clear that Noah was on the loose somewhere in the zoo! And with Noah on the loose in the zoo, anything was still possible.

"We've got to find him!" Morgan said.

"Where would you hide if you were an evil ferret?" Milton asked.

"I wouldn't be an evil ferret," Morgan told him. "I would be a kindly koala."

"I'd be a considerate kinkajou," Milton said.

"Or maybe I'd be a friendly flamingo,"

Morgan added, standing on one foot to demonstrate.

"Well, I'd be a super-hero substitute," Mrs. Worthy said. "And I'd start by using the Evil Detector 3000. It's the latest in evil-detection technology!"

Mrs. Worthy plucked what looked like an ordinary hairbrush from her purse—but when

she twisted the handle, the bristles started vibrating.

"The Evil Detector 3000 can seek out evil in a flash. It's also quite effective for styling my hair on the go!"

Milton and Morgan followed Mrs. Worthy
and her Evil Detector into the zoo. All eyes were
on the bristles of the hairbrush. Like a game of
hot and cold, the bristles reacted as the brush
sensed that they were closer and closer to evil.
Until . . .

. . . the bristles whizzed and whirred and lit
up right outside the lions' den.

"There!" Mrs. Worthy said as she turned off the hairbrush. "Without question, the horrible, hideous, disgraceful, disgustingly evil Noah is right there . . . in the lions' den."

"So all we have to do is go into the lions' den and catch him, Mrs. W.?" Morgan wanted to know.

"Exactly," Mrs. Worthy said.

"Um, Mom, I don't think that's a good idea. Look at that sign," Milton told her.

WARNING.

DO NOT ENTER THE LIONS' DEN FOR ANY REASON. THESE ARE FEROCIOUS BEASTS AND YOU MUST STAY AWAY FROM THEM **AT ALL TIMES.**

Especially if you are trying to capture an evil ferret.

Milton's mother read the sign.

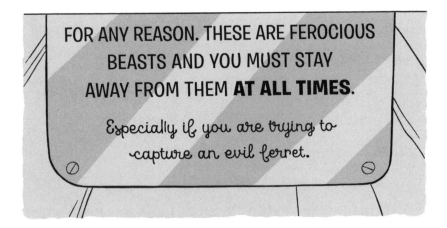

FOR ANY REASON. THESE ARE FEROCIOUS
BEASTS AND YOU MUST STAY
AWAY FROM THEM **AT ALL TIMES**.

*Especially if you are trying to
capture an evil ferret.*

She had an immediate response: "I will say that even though he's terribly evil, Noah has excellent handwriting. Look at how beautifully curved his Ss and Cs are!"

"Yeah, Mom, that's lovely if you're a substitute teacher," Milton told her. "But what about reacting as a superhero to what the sign *says*?"

"I understand why you are upset, Milty,"

Mrs. Worthy said. "But please don't fear; at the Society of Substitutes, we have two mottos . . ."

"Yes, Mom?" Milton wanted to know.

"One: no problem is too big to overcome if you've got the brainpower of a superhero."

Milton nodded.

"What's the second motto, Mrs. Worthy?" Morgan asked.

"No problem is too big to overcome if you've got . . ."

The Red Laser

". . . the tools of a substitute teacher!"

"Yay, Mom!" Milton cheered, though he was not at all sure what her plan was. (Or if she even had one.)

"Clearly, we can't just march into the lions' den to capture Noah. So here's my three-point, can't-miss idea . . ."

Mrs. Worthy huddled with the kids and shared her plan just as you'd see someone share a secret in the movies.

"Whisper, whisper, bzzz, bzzz, bzzz, bzzz, bzzz," Mrs. Worthy said.

"Mom, you're just saying the words *whisper* and *bzzz* over and over," Milton pointed out.

"Oh yes, sorry," Mrs. Worthy said. "That's how I've seen it done in the movies."

Mrs. Worthy then shared the information that, as a substitute teacher, she knew quite a lot about cats. And lions were, after all, big cats.

"Tell me, kids, what do cats like best of all?" Mrs. Worthy challenged.

"Catnip?"

"Scratching posts?"

"Ballet?"

"YouTube videos?"

"No, the simple answer is cats love chasing things. Step one: I'll pull out the laser pointer I use in class and distract them!" Mrs. Worthy said.

And that's just what she did. Aiming the pinpoint-sized red laser beam into the lions'

den, she got the attention of the ferocious creatures. She squiggled and swirled the light beam around, finally stopping high on a remote corner of the den. All the lions then bunched up into that corner, trying to "catch" the beam.

"I know what's next! I know what's next!" Milton said.

"What's that, dear?" his mother asked.

"Step two!"

"Exactly! The lions are out of the way. Now we need to draw Noah out from his hiding place," Mrs. Worthy informed the pair. "Good thing I brought along my Official S.O.S. Num-Num Launcher."

"Num-Num Launcher?" Morgan questioned.

"Certainly. It may look like an ordinary highlighter, but it's actually a device to launch tasty treats. I carry it because you never know when you need to attract an evil ferret's attention."

With her left hand, Mrs. Worthy kept the lions at bay with the laser beam. With her right hand, she used her special S.O.S. spring-loaded highlighter to fling num-nums into the lions' den.

And then ... nothing ...

"It didn't work, Mom," Milton said sadly. "Noah's not taking the bait."

And then the trio heard a sound that changed everything ...

What do you think happens next?

1 2 3 4 5 6 7 ☐ ☐ ☐ ☐

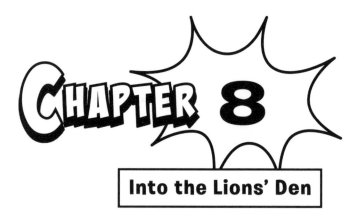

Into the Lions' Den

"Chitter-chitter."

The sound was soft. But it was just what Mrs. Worthy was waiting, and hoping, to hear . . .

"Chitter-chitter-chitter-chit."

And then . . .

"Chitter-chitter-chitter-chit-chit-mucky-freg."

Mrs. Worthy and the kids watched Noah slowly emerge from his hiding spot. He couldn't resist the pile of nummy goodness that had landed in the lions' den.

Noah scurried up to the mound of treats, licked his lips, and started gumming.

While Noah was distracted, Mrs. Worthy aimed her cell phone at the creature. Then she pressed a button to trigger the built-in Extend-A-Matic Ferret Auto-Grabber. In the blink of an eye, a cage on a giant rod zipped out of the phone. It reached all the way into the lions' den and trapped Noah.

"You got him! Yeah, Mom!" Milton yelled.

"Yes, you got him! Nice work, Mom," Morgan echoed, before correcting herself. "I mean, Mrs. Worthy."

"Thank you both." Mrs. Worthy smiled as she reeled in Noah's cage out of the lions' den.

The cage stopped right at her feet, and she double-triple locked it to keep Noah securely behind bars. She then popped up the easy-carry handle so she could tote the caged ferret around the zoo.

Just then, Zookeeper Alice and the class walked by. Mrs. Worthy told Milton and

Morgan to join the others on their zoo tour, and she'd meet them in a moment.

Once they were gone, Mrs. Worthy brought Noah back to the bus and asked Fritz to watch him. Glad to be getting his uniform back, and seeing that Noah was safely behind bars, Fritz agreed.

The rest of the zoo visit went pretty much as expected. The kids saw all the exhibits.

Sarah and Max took selfies with some of the peacock. And David traded his peanut butter sandwich for a bunch of bananas. Both he and the gorilla were quite pleased.

The only real disappointment came when some of the kids wanted to buy helium balloons. See, the buffalo had bought all of them from the zebra earlier in the day, and he simply refused to sell any to the kids.

At the end of the tour, Mrs. Worthy and the kids thanked Zoo-keeper Alice. She told them they were welcome at the zoo anytime. But she also asked them to please not come back for a few weeks.

"After the day I've had, I'm planning a long vacation. A very long vacation."

Then the second-grade class from Beacher Elementary School went back to their bus. This time, they found . . .

CHAPTER 9

High Fives!

. . . **Fritz the bus** driver, back in his uniform, standing outside the bus door to greet the class after their zoo tour. He gave a high five to each kid, and he even gave a double high five to Mrs. Worthy. And as she boarded the bus, Fritz whispered that Noah was in his cage, safely tucked inside the luggage compartment.

"Let's see how he likes the potholes on the expressway," Fritz said, smiling.

Once the kids and their superhero substitute teacher were in their seats, Fritz hopped behind the wheel. He announced, "Next stop, Beacher Elementary School! Enjoy the ride, kids!"

Compared to the zoo visit, the ride home was pretty uneventful. Milton could have sat next to any of his friends. And yet . . . he chose a seat next to his mom. Morgan did the same. (Why sit with any old second grader when you could sit with a true superhero who'd just saved the world?)

"Mom, you did it again," Milton said to his mom. "You're pretty awesome!"

"Thank you, Milton," Mrs. Worthy said, blushing a little. "So, what did you learn today?"

"Learn?" Milton asked. "Um, a bunch of random animal facts, I guess."

"Yes," Morgan agreed. "Like . . . we learned that a group of twelve or more cows is called a *flink*."

"Right, a flink," Milton said. "I like that word."

"Wait a minute, you two," Mrs. Worthy said. "I can think of quite a few other things you learned."

"Like what, Mrs. Worthy?" Morgan asked.

"Well," Milton's mom said, "you learned that solving a problem takes brainpower."

"I guess we did," Milton said.

"You learned that a substitute teacher has many tools in her arsenal."

"Yes, you're right," Morgan told her.

"You also learned that good always triumphs over evil," Mrs. Worthy told the kids. "And you learned that, just when things look darkest, you need to make a plan."

Milton thought about all that. Based on what had happened at the zoo, he had to admit that his mother was right about everything. Morgan nodded her agreement as well.

"Mom, I just thought of one more thing that we learned. And it's something I'll never, ever forget."

"What's that, dear?" Mrs. Worthy asked her son.

"We learned that Fritz the bus driver wears polka-dotted underwear!"

Mrs. Worthy laughed. It was the kind of laugh that a superhero substitute teacher parent doesn't usually laugh in front of her son.

Only two more chapters to go! Great job!

1 2 3 4 5 6 7 8 9 ☐ ☐

CHAPTER 10

One Hundred Words of Wisdom

After they returned to school, everything was back to normal in Milton's classroom at Beacher Elementary.

Mrs. Worthy had gotten off the bus first. And, with Fritz's help, she had brought the *real* Noah back where he belonged. She put him back where Electro-Replace-a-Ferret Model 602 had been. Then she invited the kids back into their classroom.

Mrs. Worthy knew that the students had been through a lot. But she also knew that they couldn't just sit there and do nothing for the final hour of the day. So, being a good substitute teacher . . .

…she told them each to write a one-hundred-word composition titled, "My Exciting Day at the Zoo."

Many kids groaned. Some slumped in their chairs. And others asked questions . . .

Mrs. Worthy smiled at all the questions, but she repeated firmly that she wanted them to write. And write they did . . .

Name: David Tessler

I went to the zoo. It was boring. Very boring. Except when the animals ran wild and took over the zoo. That was kind of cool.

Name: <u>Sarah Rosario</u>

My class went to the zoo. It was cloudy. The zookeeper's name is Alice, and she talks a lot. Mostly about animals. She has worked at the zoo for seven years. Or maybe since she was seven. I wasn't really listening.

Name: <u>Nancy Gillespie</u>

Have you ever been to the zoo?
I have. It's called a zoo because they
have zoo animals there.

Name: Max Goen

My composition is called "My Exciting Day
at the Zoo" because my substitute teacher,
Mrs. Worthy, said we have to write a
composition called "My Exciting Day at the
Zoo." My day at the zoo actually wasn't
very exciting. If I had my choice, I would
just call it "My Day at the Zoo"—and totally
leave out the word "exciting." I would also
spend more time looking at the penguins,
and I wouldn't have nachos for lunch.
Then I could probably write a truthful
composition. With the word "exciting," not
so much. There—I wrote
100 words. I'm done.

81

Name: <u>Milton Worthy</u>

Lots of kids think that ~~they're~~ their mothers
are superheroes. But mine ~~actaully~~ actually is a
superhero. No, really. She's a real-life,
save-the-world superhero. I could tell
you more, much more, but I couldn't
do it in just 100 words. It would take
1,000. Or maybe even
1,000,000. That's
how super she is.

82

Mrs. Worthy enjoyed reading each and every one of the compositions. And she especially liked Milton's. She didn't even mind that he only wrote fifty-one words. And though she gave him a D for his misspellings, he got an A+ + + + + + + + + + + + + + + + + + + in her heart for being a truly terrific son.

CHAPTER 11

Chitter-Chitter-Blotz

It's midnight. Everyone has gone home, and

in Room 311B, Mrs. Baltman's desk is waiting for her healthy return in the morning.

Everything is calm, peaceful, and silent at Beacher Elementary School.

Well, *almost* everything.

See, there's a single figure stirring inside of 311B. More specifically, a figure *inside a cage* inside 311B.

As you've probably guessed . . .

. . . it's Noah.

He is furious that he was outfoxed (or really, outferreted) on the zoo trip. But he's still seeking world domination, so he's busily cooking up a new plan that he thinks is absolutely brilliant.

This time, he's sure it will work.

But please do not be concerned. Mrs. Worthy and Milton made sure Noah was securely behind bars before they went home. So no matter how creative a plan Noah is planning to hatch . . .

. . . no matter how many he times he yells, "Chitter-chitter-blotz-glud" . . .

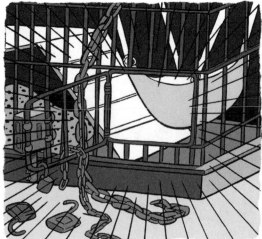

. . . there's absolutely, 100 percent no way he can escape from his ca . . .

Hey you, ferret! Get back here! Get back here right now!

Uh-oh.

SUPER AWESOME GAMES

Think

The class is going on a field trip to the
zoo. If you could take a field trip anywhere,
where would you go? Write a letter saying
why you think this would be a great trip for your class!

Feel

Milton was surprised to find out that
Noah had driven the bus to the zoo.
Can you think of a time when you did
something no one thought you could do? Draw a picture
of that moment.

Act

In this story, Mrs. Worthy stops Noah
by feeding him num-nums. What's your
favorite food? Can you create a menu for a
restaurant that serves all the things you love to eat?

Alan Katz has written more than forty books, including *Take Me Out of the Bathtub and Other Silly Dilly Songs*, *The Day the Mustache Took Over*, *OOPS!*, and *Really Stupid Stories for Really Smart Kids*. He has received many awards for his writing, and he loves visiting schools across the country.

Alex Lopez was born in Sabadell, a city in Spain near Barcelona. Alex has always loved to draw. His work has been featured in many books in many countries, but nowadays, he focuses mostly on illustrating books for young readers and teens.